GAME ON!

PASS FOR THE BASKET

BY BRANDON TERRELL

12 STORY LIBRARY

www.12StoryLibrary.com

Copyright © 2015 by Peterson Publishing Company, North Mankato, MN 56003. All rights reserved. No part of this book may be reproduced or utilized in any form or by any means without written permission from the publisher.

12-Story Library is an imprint of Peterson Publishing Company and Press Room Editions.

Produced for 12-Story Library by Red Line Editorial

Photographs ©: Shutterstock Images, cover

Cover Design: Nikki Farinella

ISBN
978-1-63235-049-7 (hardcover)
978-1-63235-109-8 (paperback)
978-1-62143-090-2 (hosted ebook)

Library of Congress Control Number: 2014946010

Printed in the United States of America
Mankato, MN
October, 2014

TABLE OF CONTENTS

CHAPTER 1

A DRAMATIC ENDING

Ben Mason dribbled to midcourt and glanced up at the scoreboard on the gymnasium's wall. In bright red numerals, the time left on the clock clicked down.

0:47 . . . 0:46 . . . 0:45 . . .

It was the fourth quarter, and Ben's team, the East Grover Lake Grizzlies, was down by 3 points. The Grizzlies were playing a team from Naperville, the gold-and-white-clad Gladiators. The Gladiators were a fast team. They'd been running circles around

4

the Grizzlies the whole second half. Ben was amazed that the Grizzlies were just a few points down as the seconds ticked away.

From the sideline, Ben heard Coach Horton shout, "Bear Cub! Bear Cub!"

As point guard for the Grizzlies, Ben's job was to run the plays. He had to make sure all the players knew their positions, where they had to be for each play, and who they should pass the ball to at any given moment.

Basically, Ben was in charge. This was his team. He liked that.

"Go Grizzlies, go!" shouted Ben's friends in the stands. Annie Roger and Gabe Santiago, dressed in their red and brown school colors, cheered him on. He could hear them over the clapping of the crowd and the chanting of the cheerleaders. Ben's other close friend, Logan

Parrish, was on the bench. Logan was one of the Grizzlies' forwards.

"Bear Cub!" Ben shouted to his teammates as he reached the top of the key. The Gladiators' defender played close, but not *too* close. A foul would send Ben to the free-throw line, and the Gladiators didn't want to give away any easy points.

Nick Cozzetti, one of the Grizzlies' forwards, dashed up and set a pick. Ben breezed past the defender and dribbled into the lane. The player defending Tyler Murphy, the Grizzlies' center, peeled off to defend the driving Ben. That left Ty wide open.

Ben bounce-passed to Ty, who drained an easy layup.

"Nice pass!" Ty shouted as he and Ben slapped a high five.

The Grizzlies were now down by 1 point.

"No time to celebrate!" Coach Horton waved an arm animatedly. "Foul! Foul!"

Coach Horton wanted them to intentionally foul to stop the clock. Ben hazarded a look at the ticking clock.

0:25 . . . 0:24 . . . 0:23 . . .

Aware of the Grizzlies' intentions, the Gladiators sent the inbound pass to their best shooter, Carl Martinson. He snatched the ball and held it tight as Ben swatted at his arm.

Tweet!

The referee pointed at Ben. "Foul! Two shots, Gladiators."

The teams lined up on both sides of the lane. As Carl toed the free-throw line, waiting to get the ball from the ref, the Grizzlies' fans in the crowd began to stomp their feet on the wooden bleachers. A low rumble resonated throughout the gymnasium.

The ref passed Carl the ball. He dribbled twice, spun the ball in his hand, and shot.

The ball rattled around the rim and then dropped in.

Down by two points, Ben thought. He hoped the home crowd would rattle Carl on his next attempt.

Carl received the ball again. He took a deep breath, went through his routine, and shot.

This time, the ball bounced high off the rim and fell toward a mass of leaping bodies and outstretched arms.

Ty came down with the rebound.

0:13 . . . 0:12 . . . 0:11 . . .

Ty found Nick open at midcourt and slung a pass up to him. Ben ran as hard as he could along the far side of the court. His team didn't have much time to get a shot off before the buzzer sounded.

0:08 . . . 0:07 . . . 0:06 . . .

Nick caught the pass at midcourt and spun. There was an open player near the top of the 3-point line. Nick passed the ball . . .

. . . and it was deflected by a Gladiator defender. The ball bounced back toward Ben.

0:04 . . . 0:03 . . . 0:02 . . .

Ben quickly snatched up the ball. He was steps from the 3-point line. There was no time to set up. As a Gladiator defender rushed toward him, Ben leaped up and shot the ball in a high, beautiful arc. The defender tried to swat away the shot, but he missed by inches.

As Ben watched the ball sail toward the hoop, the buzzer echoed across the gym. The crowd held its collective breath.

The ball hit the front of the rim, bounced high, ricocheted off the backboard, rattled around the rim, and then . . . dropped right through the hoop.

"Yes!" Ben pumped a fist in the air as the other Grizzlies swarmed around him. The crowd jumped from their seats and went wild.

Ben smiled wide as he took it all in.

He'd done it. He'd won the game.

CHAPTER 2

EXCITING NEWS

The following afternoon, as practice was about to start, the Grizzlies were still riding high on their exciting, last-second win. Some of the players stood in a circle and passed a ball to one another while chatting about Ben's game-winning shot. A few were running sprints back and forth across the gym, their feet slapping and squeaking against the wood floor. Ben and Logan were among some players practicing free throws. Coach Horton was still in the locker room.

"Hey guys! Check it out!" Ty walked into the gym, waving wildly with one arm.

Ty held his phone out in front of him. Players huddled around him as he said, "My buddy Jace sent this to me."

Ben walked up and stood in the back of the crowd. He craned his neck to see the phone's small screen.

A shaky video began to play. It was footage from the game. Jace's voice could be heard saying, "Oh man, this is intense. Grizzlies down by two." On the court, the Gladiator player was missing his second free throw.

"Okay, here it is," Ty said. The ball was passed down the court, was deflected, and landed in Ben's hands. He took a step and shot it at the last second.

"Whoooooaaaa!" Jace said as the buzzer sounded and the shot went in. "I can't believe he hit that! Grizzlies win!"

The Grizzlies' players echoed Jace's excitement as Ty replayed the video. They watched it again. Then again. And then one more time. "Ben Mason for the win!" one of the team's forwards, a kid named Wesley Trask, said. He punched Ben lightly on the shoulder. Ben grinned and puffed his chest out a little more than usual.

"What's the big hubbub?" Coach Horton's voice filled the whole gym. He was a short man with broad shoulders and a muscular physique. He was the exact opposite of his older brother, Sal, who owned the used sporting goods store that Ben and his friends often visited. Sal was a towering man with a graying beard and a barrel chest.

"We're watching Ben hit that 3-pointer from yesterday," Ty said.

"Well, put it away," Coach Horton barked. "Yesterday's over. Time to get ready for our next game."

Ty did as he was told, stuffing the phone into his gym bag behind the bench.

Coach Horton said, "All right, before we get started, I've got an announcement to make." The team looked at one another, a mixture of curiosity and concern on their faces. "It looks like we'll be welcoming a new Grizzly to our squad this week. A transfer student from Maxfield Prep."

"Maxfield Prep?" Logan said. "That school produces some of the best basketball players in the state."

Maxfield was a few hours from Grover Lake and in a higher division than the Grizzlies, but everyone knew about its team. It had won the state championship last year.

"Who is it?" Ty asked.

"Carter Cressman," Coach Horton replied.

Ben had heard of him. He was a shooting guard and one of Maxfield's top scorers. Judging by the gasps of disbelief from his teammates, Ben wasn't the only who was familiar with Carter's abilities.

"No way," Nick said. "Carter Cressman is transferring to our school?"

"He is," Coach Horton explained. "His family just moved to town, and his first day is tomorrow. He'll be at our next practice."

Ben's stomach dropped as he realized what all that meant. His time to revel in the limelight of yesterday's victory was over. When their new teammate took the court beside him, the focus would be on Carter, one of the state's best players.

"All right!" Coach Horton blasted a loud chirp from his whistle. "Everyone on the baseline! Five killers on my mark!"

As the team ran up and down the court—foul line, back, half-court, back, far foul line, back, baseline, back—Ben tried to shake the sense of impending doom he felt from Carter's arrival. He couldn't, though. Things were going to change for the Grizzlies, for Ben especially.

Would it still be his offense to run? he wondered. *Or would this be Carter's team?*

Ben was distracted the entire practice. He missed easy passes and messed up on some shooting drills. At one point, Coach

Horton blew his whistle and said, "Mason, take a breather. Peterson, you're running point." Blake Peterson, a backup point guard, replaced Ben. Ben sat on the bench, a towel over his face, trying not to let his emotions get the best of him.

After practice, as the team changed in the locker room, players were still abuzz about their new team member.

"Guys, you've gotta see this," Ty said. He was sitting on the metal bench in front of his locker, scrolling through his phone again, looking at a video online.

This time, though, it was a video of Carter Cressman.

"This is from Maxfield Prep's championship game last season," he explained as some of the other players hovered over him.

"Hey, Ben," Logan said as he leaned over Ty's left shoulder. "You gotta see this."

"No thanks." Ben slid his jacket on, snatched his backpack out of his locker, and slammed it closed.

He walked out of the locker room just as his team let out resounding cries of "Whoa!" and "Amazing!" and "I can't wait to play with him!"

CHAPTER 3

THE NEW KID

**"Dude, Carter Cressman is *in the building*,"
Logan said as he slid into the chair across
from Ben in the school's cafeteria.** Annie and
Gabe were also there with him.

Ben was snacking on a granola bar and
sipping on a bottle of orange juice from the
vending machine. The first morning bell was
still 10 minutes from ringing.

"Who?" Gabe looked up from the thick
science textbook resting before him on
the table.

"The new kid from Maxfield Prep," Annie explained. "He's a crazy-good basketball player. Also, I hear he's kind of cute."

Logan rolled his eyes.

"Ty saw him go into the office this morning, probably to get his class schedule or something. He hasn't come out yet, though."

Ben glanced across the cafeteria. From their table, the glass door to the principal's office could be seen down one of the far halls. A few of the players from the basketball team—Nick, Ty, and Wesley—were loitering around the door.

It's like they're waiting for an autograph from LeBron James or something, Ben thought.

When the bell rang, the four friends
gathered their things and headed off to class.
Ben gave one last look back at the principal's
office, but no one emerged.

It wasn't until third period that Ben
finally laid eyes on Carter. Ben was in Mr.
May's geometry class, and Annie was at
the desk next to him. They were waiting for
the bell to ring when the new kid walked in
the door.

Carter was tall with black hair that
swooped down almost to his eyes. He
seemed somewhat awkward, almost unsure
of himself, as he approached Mr. May.

"Ah, you must be Mr. Cressman," Mr. May said, adjusting his glasses. He waved with one hand. "Please, find an open seat."

There was a desk open to Ben's left, and Carter dropped into it. He looked over, noticed Ben, and said, "Hey, you're on the b-ball team, aren't you?"

Ben's answer was a succinct "Yep."

"Ben Mason, right?"

"Yep."

"Cool. I already met Coach Horton. He seems like an okay guy."

Ben nodded. Sure, it seemed like Carter was just trying to be friendly, but Ben was super annoyed by the guy. He willed the bell to ring.

"Psst!" Annie whispered, leaning close to Ben. "Introduce me."

"Not now," Ben shot back.

Brriinnnng!

Mr. May rubbed his hands together. "All right, class. Let's get started. Who's ready to discover the beauty of the Pythagorean theorem?"

After school, Ben was the first player to suit up and hit the court. He shot a few hoops by himself, chasing down his own rebounds and lofting easy layups off the backboard. It was the calm before the storm, and he wanted to enjoy the last few moments of peace before Hurricane Carter struck.

Carter walked out of the locker room surrounded by his new teammates. Ben was surprised—*well, not really*—to see his friend Logan among them.

"Welcome to the team," Nick said.

"With you, we're going to win our division," said Blake.

Carter grabbed a ball off a nearby metal rack and dribbled onto the court. He nodded and said, "Hey, Ben. Good to see ya, man."

"Hey." Ben shot a jumper, and it clanged off the rim.

Soon, Coach Horton joined them. He carried a rolled-up red spiral notebook in one hand.

"Okay, fellas," he said after they'd completed their warm-ups. "We've got a big game coming up against Hightower. I've made a few changes to our motion offense, so let's get down to it. Ben!"

Ben jogged over to the top of the key, ball in hand.

"Ty, you're under the hoop. Logan and Nick, on the sides. And Carter . . ."

"Yeah, Coach?"

"On Ben's left. We're throwing you right into the mix. Got it?"

"Thanks, Coach."

Ugh, what a suck-up, Ben thought.

Coach Horton ran them through a play they called Red Paw. In the end, the ball is passed back to Ben, who drives to the hoop and shoots.

As Ben caught the pass and started his drive, Coach Horton called out, "Now pass to Carter, Ben."

Ben was taken aback. "Wait," he said. "This is my play. I'm supposed to shoot."

Coach shook his head. "Not anymore. The ball's going back outside now."

Annoyed, Ben did as he was told. Carter put up the shot, and it *swished* through the hoop.

It turned out that almost all of Coach Horton's "revised" plays were just the same plays they'd run before, only now Ben passed the ball off to Carter. Ben's role on the court had changed. He was still the point guard, still called the plays, still ran the offense, but the Grizzlies were Carter's team now.

CHAPTER 4

TIP-OFF

The Grizzlies' next game was played in Hightower, against the home team Rebels. The bus ride over was chilly—the outside temperatures had dipped below freezing the night before—but inside, the gymnasium was sweltering.

As the team walked in, bags on shoulders, the heat nearly bowled Ben over. "Oh man, are they trying to cook us?" he asked, shedding his coat.

"Don't think about it," Coach Horton said. "Stay mentally prepared. Got it, Mason?"

"Yes, Coach," Ben said.

The team used a small guest locker room to change into their uniforms and sneakers. Then they filed out onto the court to warm up.

Usually, the stands for the middle school games were sparsely filled until the second half. The junior varsity teams faced off after the first game was finished. When they were done, the varsity teams took the court to a packed audience.

This afternoon, though, the stands were already filling in, especially on the Grizzlies' side of the gym. Hightower was not too far from Grover Lake, and many had taken the trip to see the team's new player.

Ben saw Annie and Gabe sitting among a group of students. Annie waved to him, but he didn't return the favor. He also saw Sal, seated in the front row, right behind the bench. The shop owner was wearing a Grizzlies ball cap and munching on a bag of popcorn from the concession stand.

The orange-and-purple-clad Rebels warmed up on the far side of the court. Ben caught a couple of the players watching Carter practicing layups. Whether they were intimidated or jealous, Ben couldn't tell.

The teams lined up for introductions, which were done over a small sound system pumped through speakers on the wall by the scoreboard. As each name was called, starting with the visiting team, the player jogged out to midcourt and waited for his teammates. Typically, the point guard was announced last. That's why Ben was surprised when his name came up fourth.

"Point guard, Ben Mason," the announcer said. There was a round of applause as Ben trotted onto the court.

Then the announcer shouted, "And shooting guard for the Grizzlies, Carter Cressman!" The Grizzlies' crowd cheered louder than Ben had ever heard them at an away game. Carter jogged out, waving to the stands like he was a celebrity or something.

After that, the Rebels' players were announced, and the home crowd cheered wildly.

Ty and the Rebels' center met for the tip-off.

Tweeet!

The ref blew his whistle and tossed the ball high into the air. Ty leaped up and batted the ball back.

Right into Carter's hands.

Carter passed to Ben, who brought the ball up the court. He waited until the rest of his teammates were in position, and then called for a play known as Grizzly Attack.

Ty set a screen for Ben, who dribbled right, cut to the free-throw line, and dished the ball off to Carter on the far side of the court. Carter was double-covered, but he still managed to get off a shot.

Swish!

The Grizzlies' fans loved it.

And they had a lot to cheer about during the first half, since nearly every play was identical to that one. Ben put up a few shots when he was open, but only one of them fell. The rest were either tipped in by Ty or rebounded by the Rebels.

Meanwhile, Carter was a scoring machine. He played almost every minute of the half, like he'd been an integral part of the team from the beginning of the season.

The Rebels stuck with them, though. They had a couple of great role players, or players with specific skills who could come off the bench when needed. One of them, a tall and lanky guard named Zimmerman, drained almost every 3-pointer he shot.

When the buzzer sounded at the end of the first half, the score was tied, 34-34.

CHAPTER 5

IT ALL FALLS APART

"Great job out there," Coach Horton said, clipboard tucked under one arm. The players were seated in the locker room, catching their breath and drinking from red squirt bottles. "Our new plays are working great," Coach continued. "Just keep your heads in the game, and we can win this thing."

Ben wiped his dripping forehead with an equally sweaty arm. He glanced over at Carter, who looked like he'd been sitting on the bench all game.

Man, how is he not sweating? Ben thought. *That gym is hotter than a sauna. I feel like I've lost five pounds already.*

"All right, bring it in!" Coach stretched out one hand, and each team member placed a hand on top of it. Ben was the second-to-last player to join in. Carter sidled in next to him and slapped his hand onto Ben's. "Go Grizzlies, on three. One . . . two . . . three!"

"Go Grizzlies!"

The second half picked up right where the first left off. The two teams were well matched. When the Grizzlies went on a scoring run, sinking five shots in a row and taking a 10-point lead, the Rebels came roaring back.

Carter continued to be a machine. After hitting a hook shot to give the Grizzlies the lead again, he jogged past Ben and said, "Nice pass, Mason."

Ben's blood boiled. *That's it*, he thought. *Carter shouldn't get all the glory.*

The Rebels' point guard brought the ball to the top of the key. He passed off to a forward, who searched around for an open man. Ben read the forward's eyes and knew he was going to pass back to the guard.

When he did, Ben leaped in front of the ball and swatted it away.

He gained control of it and dribbled down the court on a breakaway. Darting along a few steps ahead of him was Carter. Between them was the Rebels' center.

And he was blocking Ben's path to the basket.

Carter waved his hands frantically. "I'm open! I'm open!"

The smart play is to pass the ball, Ben thought. Then, he quickly decided, *Forget that*. Ben ignored Carter's cries. He dribbled for the hoop, put up the shot . . .

. . . and it was rejected by the center.

A murmur of disappointment swelled through the Grizzlies' fans. Ben could see the frustration on Coach Horton's face as the man yelled, "Go! Get back on D!"

Toward the end of the fourth quarter, the Grizzlies were down by one point. Ben glanced up at the clock.

0:15 . . . 0:14 . . . 0:13 . . .

"Time-out!" a ref yelled.

From the bench, Coach Horton had flashed his hands in a T signal.

The Hightower cheerleaders led the crowd in a fight song as the two teams went to their benches. Ben and the other Grizzlies huddled around Coach Horton, who crouched down on one knee.

"We've got one shot here," he said, scribbling on a small whiteboard with a marker. He placed an X where each Grizzlies player was to go, and an O for each Rebel.

Ben watched as Coach explained a double pick, a sweep under the hoop by

Carter, a pass by Ben, and a jump shot that *should* give the Grizzlies a win. It was a cut-and-dried play.

And, of course, it ended with Carter taking the shot.

Nick passed the ball in to Ben from the sideline. Ben dribbled quickly into position and watched as the team began the final play.

The double pick was executed perfectly.

Carter ran beneath the hoop and came out the other side.

Ben lined up to pass . . .

. . . and then his defender backed off a step, giving him space to shoot.

0:04 . . . 0:03 . . . 0:02 . . .

What do you think of this,
Carter Cressman?

Ben leaped into the air and shot the ball.
The buzzer sounded.

Clang!

The shot was wide, striking the side of
the rim and falling right into Carter's arms.
A look of confused disbelief washed over
his face.

The game was over, and the Grizzlies
had lost.

CHAPTER **6**

HIDING OUT

The locker room was dead silent, aside from the shuffling of feet and the occasional cough or sniffle. None of the Grizzlies talked about the loss, but Ben could feel them glaring at his back as he peeled off his sweat-soaked jersey and crammed it into his duffel bag. He just wanted to go home and hide, forever.

Usually, the team hung around and watched the JV and varsity teams play, as a sign of solidarity. But Ben's parents were somewhere in the crowd, and they wouldn't have a problem cutting out early if he wanted to. And he did.

He was just about to leave, had his coat on and everything, when Nick said, "Man, you should have passed the ball."

Ben stopped. He could feel the color rising into his cheeks. He turned to Nick and looked around. His teammates were watching to see what he would do or say. Ben glanced over at Logan, waiting for his friend to stick up for him.

Logan stared at his sneakers and said nothing.

Ben took a deep breath through his nose, filled his nostrils with the awful smell of the locker room, and started to walk away again.

"Did you hear me, Ben?" Nick's voice was louder now. "We could have won the game if you had passed the ball to Carter."

That's it.

Ben strode back toward Nick. He could feel his hand curling into a fist. His anger was boiling over.

"I had an open shot," Ben scowled.

"What's going on here?" Coach Horton asked as he suddenly appeared behind Nick. Ben stopped in his tracks.

"Nothing," Ben said.

Then he turned on his heel, banged through the locker room door, and stepped out into the gymnasium, where the JV game was already under way.

I wanna go home.

It was close to midnight when something struck Ben's bedroom window.

Ting!

It startled him as he was still awake. He was laying on his bed and reading an article about Chris Paul—his favorite NBA point guard, who played for the Los Angeles Clippers. Ben was also trying his best not to think about the Grizzlies' loss earlier that night. He wore a pair of plaid flannel pants and a Clippers sweatshirt.

Ting!

Ben's face scrunched up in confusion.

What was that?

He rolled off his bed and looked out just as a pebble struck the glass.

Ting!

His heart nearly climbed out of his throat. He ducked as if the next rock would crush his skull.

A moment passed. Then Ben hazarded a quick glance out the window. In the pool of light cast from a nearby street lamp, he saw Annie waving at him.

He cracked open the window, letting in a rush of cold air.

"Are you crazy?" Ben scolded Annie. "You could have broken my window!"

"I would have sent you a text but my phone's dead," Annie said. "Come down."

"Why? It's super late."

"Just do it."

Annie's family lived across the street, just a few houses away. She and Ben had been friends since the two of them used to have tricycle races down the sidewalk and compete in marathon games of hide-and-seek.

Ben stepped quietly out into the hall. His parents were already fast asleep. He tiptoed down the carpeted stairs, slid on a pair of battered sneakers, and fetched a stocking cap from the front closet. Then he slipped out the door and joined Annie in the front yard.

"So what's going on with you?" Annie asked. "Gabe and I looked for you after the game, but Logan said you bailed."

"Nothing."

Annie wasn't buying it.

"Right! I've known you my whole life. You can't lie to me."

"It's just . . . everyone's getting pulled into Carter Cressman's stupid gravitational orbit. You included, and I'm feeling left out."

"What? I haven't—"

Ben batted his eyelashes. His voice went up an octave as he imitated Annie. "Carter is *soooo* cute."

Annie rolled her eyes and hit him in the chest. "That sounds nothing like me."

"After the game, Nick said we'd have won if Carter had taken the shot instead of me."

"How does he know that? Is he, like, a psychic or something?"

"Carter's good. Really good. I don't know, I just . . . I liked being the team leader."

"You still are," Annie said as she pretended to dribble an imaginary ball down the driveway. She faked a pass to Ben and then pretended to shoot. "You're the glue, man. Without Ben Mason, the team falls apart."

"I guess."

"Guess? I know. What do you say we set up a game over at Grover Park Sunday? You, me, Gabe, Logan, and Ty. Invite Carter too."

"You'd like that, wouldn't you?"

Annie smiled. "Shut it, Mason."

"Yeah," Ben said. "Yeah, that could be fun. Besides, I really don't know much about the guy. Maybe it would help."

"It will. I promise." Annie shivered from the cold. "All right, I gotta go. It's freezing out here. I have no idea why you dragged me outside at this time of night."

Ben laughed. It felt good to laugh.

"Hey, thanks," he called after Annie as she walked down his driveway.

"No prob." And with that, she darted for the warm comfort of her home.

CHAPTER 7

THE WISDOM OF SAL

Sunday afternoon, Ben and Annie rode their bikes together to the basketball court in Grover Park. It was a place their friends frequented, and today, despite the overcast skies, cool breeze, and threat of snow later in the day, the park was filled with people.

Annie carried her lucky basketball with her. It used to belong to the Houston Comets, a WNBA championship team. Annie and Ben ditched their bikes against the thick trunk of an ancient oak tree and approached the empty court.

"First ones here, as usual," Annie said, dribbling the ball a bit and sinking a jump shot.

Ben scooped up the loose ball. "You think Carter will show?"

"Of course," Annie answered. "Did you text him?"

"Yeah."

They played a bit of 1-on-1 while they waited for the others. Ben enjoyed playing basketball against Annie. She was a top athlete, quick and smart. She could play circles around many of the guys her age and was the starting point guard for the Grizzlies' girls' middle school team.

Ben was just putting up a long 3-point shot when he heard a car honking. He and Annie stopped playing and looked over to the nearby street.

A white compact car, old and battered, had pulled over to the curb. The man lumbering out of the vehicle was Sal, owner of Sal's Used Sporting Goods.

Sal waved a meaty hand at them. "Greetings!"

"Hi, Sal!" Annie shouted. Ben waved.

Sal made his way over to the basketball court. He held a white towel or shirt in one hand. Ben couldn't see exactly what it was.

"I was just on my way home from the store, and saw you shooting some hoops," Sal said. Sal's Used Sporting Goods was a cluttered, dusty, wonderful, and magical place. It was located not far from Grover Park, in a small commercial section of town filled with old brick buildings.

"You're just the person I was looking for, Ben," Sal continued.

Ben was puzzled. "I am?"

"Yes. That was one heck of a game the other night. Heartbreaking loss."

"Yeah," Ben said, adding under his breath, "don't remind me."

"Don't let it get you down. My brother said you're struggling to adjust to the new player on your team."

Ben nodded.

"Well, I brought you something that may cheer you up *and* help you out."

Sal tossed Ben what he had been holding. Ben caught it, taking it in both hands and spreading it out so he could see the gift more clearly.

It was a basketball jersey, a bit faded, with bold purple letters spelling out the word *JAZZ* on it. The curl of the J was a purple-and-yellow basketball. The number 12 was emblazoned on both sides. The name on the back read STOCKTON.

"Wait," Annie said. "Is that . . . ?"

"A practice jersey once worn by John Stockton of the Utah Jazz," Sal explained.

Ben had heard of John Stockton. His dad had mentioned Stockton when he would talk about the "glory days of the NBA." Of course, Ben wasn't surprised that Annie knew who John Stockton was. Ben could see a hint of jealousy in her eyes.

"Mr. Stockton played his entire career with the Jazz," Sal explained. "He holds the NBA's record for most career assists."

"And for most steals," Annie added.

Sal smiled. "Yes. For most of his career, Stockton passed the ball to Karl Malone, aka The Mailman. They were a formidable duo."

Ben knew what Sal was getting at. "Let me guess. Only Malone had the cool nickname and scored all the points."

Sal laughed. "Yes, but that's not the point of the game, is it? Which teammate scores the most points."

Ben shook his head.

"Winning and being a team player," Sal said. "*That's* what matters. Stockton was an amazing team leader, and he's considered one of the best players in NBA history."

"Thanks, Sal." Ben slid the jersey over his head, wearing it on top of his sweatshirt.

"You've got a great team," Sal said. "So help it play like one."

With a wink and a wave, the generous shopkeeper said goodbye and walked back to his car.

CHAPTER 8

3-ON-3

"Whoa! Cool jersey, *amigo!*" Gabe said.

He and Logan arrived mere minutes after Sal had driven away. Each brought his own basketball with him. They parked their bikes by the others and joined Annie and Ben on the court.

Logan pulled Ben aside. "Hey, sorry about yesterday in the locker room," he said. "I should have stood up for you."

Ben shrugged. "It's okay."

"Nick was just upset and running his mouth. He doesn't mean it."

"I know."

Ty showed up next, climbing out of a large SUV driven by his older sister. Ben and his friends started tossing the balls around and shooting baskets.

Ben checked his watch. It was almost 15 minutes past the time he'd texted everyone to meet, and there was still no Carter Cressman.

Huh. Dude must think he's better than the rest of us, after all.

As they tried to decide who would sit out for the first game of 2-on-2, a voice behind Ben yelled out, "Sorry I'm late."

Carter strode across the grass near the court, shaky and a little out of breath.

"I walked here from my place, but I got totally turned around. Wound up making a complete circle before I figured out where I was."

"No worries," Ty said, bumping fists with Carter.

"Cool, now the teams will be even," Logan said.

"Hey, Ben." Carter held out his fist and, after a brief hesitation, Ben tapped it with his own.

Annie said, "Um . . . hi, Carter." Ben had never heard her sound so nervous. She smiled, drawing her usually wild, curly brown hair back from her face and tucking it behind her ear.

"Hi," Carter said shyly. "Annie, right? Annie Roger?"

"Yes!" Annie answered, a bit too loudly. She then added, "I mean, yeah, that's me."

"Cool."

Wait, did Carter sound just as nervous as Annie? Oh, good grief.

"So are we gonna keep saying 'hi' to each other or are we gonna play a little ball?" Logan asked.

They picked teams, and Ben wound up alongside Carter and Gabe.

Ben took the ball first. He was guarded by Annie, who crouched low and gave him the "stink-eye."

"Bring it, Mason," she said.

He dribbled to his right, where Gabe was matched up against Logan. Ben dished the ball, and then cut down the court, setting a pick and giving Gabe a chance to swing the ball to the free-throw line. Gabe bounced the ball back to Ben. Ben saw Carter break away from Ty, and he fed the ball past Annie. Carter caught the pass and gave a head fake that Ty fell for completely. The tall center leaped through the air, past Carter, who then had an easy jump shot off the backboard.

Swish.

"Two points!" Carter said. "Nice pass, B."

"Nice shot," Ben fired back, trying to stay positive.

Ben realized early on in their game that Sal and Annie were both right. It was okay to let someone else shine, because the ultimate goal was to win.

They played for almost two hours, until it was nearly dinnertime and the sun was beginning to lower in the sky. Now that winter had nearly arrived, the trees were shedding their leaves, and the sun was disappearing earlier and earlier.

Soon, the court at Grover Park would be buried under snow until next spring.

Ben sat in the grass beneath the oak tree. He was soon joined by the others.

No one spoke for a while. Then Carter said, "Thanks, guys."

"Thanks for what?" Gabe asked. "Isn't playing basketball what you do?"

"For inviting me. Sounds a little crazy, but I've actually had a hard time making friends at school. All everyone wants to talk about is basketball."

"Like, what else is there?" Annie asked.

"Like video games," Carter said. "Ever play *Werewolves vs. Zombies*?"

"Dude, that's my favorite!" Logan nearly shouted.

"Well," Ben said, "looks like you've got some friends now."

"Yeah. Yeah, I guess I do."

CHAPTER 9

BACK ON THE COURT

The following week's practices were different. After realizing how effective he could actually be as a point guard, Ben gladly resumed his role as team leader. To show his change in attitude, he wore the gift he'd gotten from Sal to each practice.

"Nice jersey, Ben," Coach Horton said. "John Stockton's a great role model for any aspiring point guard."

"Thanks, Coach."

Their next game was at home, and it was the biggest game of the season. They were playing last season's divisional champions, the Eagle Valley Cougars. The school held a pep rally at the end of the school day. The gym was filled with a sea of red and brown as students and faculty showed their Grizzly pride. Banners hung across the gym walls, with painted messages reading GRRRRRRIZZLIES! and GO! FIGHT! WIN! BEAT THE COUGARS! A small banner hung on the wall at the top of the bleachers made a powerful proclamation: I LOVE YOU, CARTER CRESSMAN!

Ben just rolled his eyes.

He saw Annie and Gabe in their usual spot up in the bleachers. Sal was there as well, seated down front, behind the bench. Tonight, he was wearing a purple Utah Jazz ball cap to go with his Grizzlies sweatshirt.

Ben nodded at him.

In return, Sal reached up and tipped his cap.

The Eagle Valley Cougars were an intimidating team. Even though they were all middle schoolers, every player wearing yellow and white looked as tall as some of the high school basketball players. They took the tip-off easily, passing the ball once, twice, three times, and then scoring.

Less than 10 seconds had ticked off the clock.

Oh boy, Ben thought, *this could be a long game.*

Nick inbounded the ball to Ben, who dribbled across the back court. He needed to control the game's tempo, to slow things down so the guys were not simply reacting to the Cougars' style of play.

"Red Paw!" he called out as he crossed midcourt.

He dished the ball off to Nick, who looked down into the paint, where Ty was fighting for position against the Cougars' center. He wasn't open, so Nick passed the ball back to Ben.

Ben drove toward the hoop, looked over at Carter, and saw that Carter was double-covered. Ben stopped and picked up his dribble instead of passing.

Bad move, he thought.

The Cougar defender was all over him. Ben twisted back and forth, trying to keep the ball away from him. Ben saw an open player and passed the ball.

It was intercepted by another Cougar, who took it all the way to the hoop for an unassisted basket.

It was an epic battle trying to keep pace with the Cougars. Carter, fighting for every inch of space between himself and his defenders, drained a couple of 3-pointers. Ty battled with elbows and determination in the paint. He was fouled several times, and wound up shooting free throws, at which he excelled—something most centers weren't good at.

Still, the Cougars had their number, and by the end of the first half, the Grizzlies were down 37-29.

CHAPTER 10

LEADING THE CHARGE

The mood in the locker room was frenzied.
The Grizzlies were panicking. Ben, though, was more frustrated than anything. He felt like he was to blame for the team's failings. He was their leader; he needed to take charge.

"Focus and ball control," Coach Horton said calmly. "Don't let them dictate how this game is played. Find the open man, and take smart shots. That's how we play. There's still an entire half of basketball. Got it?"

68

"Yes, Coach," the team said in unison.

The Grizzlies had possession of the ball after the half.

Ben brought the ball down the court. The Cougars continued to play tough defense on Carter. There was no way Ben was getting the ball to him.

Ty ran up and set a pick. Ben curled around him, looked to pass, saw no one, and took the shot instead.

The ball rattled around the rim and then fell.

"Great shot, Ben!" he heard Annie cheer from the stands.

Okay, Ben thought as he jogged back on defense, *if the Cougars think Carter is the only shooter we've got on our team, then it's time to prove them wrong.*

On the opposite end of the court, the Cougars passed the ball to their center, who banked a shot off the backboard. It ricocheted off the rim, and Ty came down with the rebound.

He passed the ball up to Ben, who led a breakaway down the court. He had Carter on his left, Nick on his right.

As he reached the key, Ben faked a pass to Carter. The defender bit, and Ben looped the ball around his back, bouncing it perfectly to Nick, who took it in stride for an easy layup.

"Whoa!" Carter said as the three boys jogged back on defense. "Trying to make the highlight reel, Mason?"

Ben smiled, and the two bumped fists.

Ben's focus was razor-sharp. Each time down the court, he found an open man—Nick in the corner for 3 points, Ty in the paint with a layup, Wesley driving toward the hoop. With the Cougars focusing so much on Carter, Ben was able to pass the ball around more. And when the defense finally loosened up on Carter, Ben fed him the ball, as well.

The Grizzlies picked away at the Cougars' lead, but time was running out.

After Carter sunk a hook shot to pull the team to within 1 point, Coach Horton shouted, "Get the ball back!"

The inbound pass was lobbed up over Ben, who was playing close to the Cougars' point guard. Ben leaped into the air, tipped the pass . . .

. . . and the ball landed in Nick's hands!

Ben glanced at the clock.

0:09 . . . 0:08 . . . 0:07 . . .

Nick fired the ball to Ben, who quickly surveyed the court. Ty was dashing down the lane, heavily covered. Wesley fought to get open. Nothing. Carter was double-covered, leaving Ben loosely guarded.

Ben drove for the hoop. He was going to have to do this by himself. He was going to have to be the hero.

0:05 . . . 0:04 . . . 0:03 . . .

He drove past the free-throw line. Two Cougars saw him and peeled off their guys to race over and block Ben's shot.

Ben brought the ball up, leaped into the air, squared up for the shot . . .

. . . and saw Carter wide open out of the corner of his eye.

In midair, Ben flung the ball with both hands. As he came back down, his foot tangled with one of the two defenders covering him, and he fell hard to the floor.

Carter caught the ball and, with milliseconds left on the clock, put up the shot.

The buzzer sounded.

The crowd waited.

Ben looked up from his spot on the hardwood.

Swish!

Nothing but net.

After the game, when the buzz inside the locker room had died down, Ben and Logan went back out into the gymnasium to find their friends. Gabe and Annie were halfway up the bleachers, surrounded by other students.

Moments after they'd climbed the steps and sat next to their friends, Ben spied Carter coming out of the locker room. Carter looked around, unsure where to go.

Ben cupped his hands around his mouth. "Carter!"

Carter climbed the steps to join them.

They watched the JV team play, laughing and joking with one another. Then, they cheered on the varsity team, who also came away with a victory. All in all, it was a great night for East Grover Lake boys' basketball.

As the crowd thinned, streaming from the bleachers while the pep band played the East Grover Lake fight song, Ben and his friends stood and stretched.

Then Logan asked, "Anybody want to hit the Lake Diner for some grub?"

"Yes, please," Annie answered.

"Count me in," Gabe said.

"What do you say, Carter?" Ben asked.

Carter nodded. "Yeah, sure. I'm starving."

"Good," Ben said as they stood up. He draped an arm around the new kid's shoulders and led him down the bleacher steps. "Because I'd like to introduce you to a little something called the Mega-chocolate Eruption milk shake."

THE END

ABOUT THE AUTHOR

Brandon Terrell is a Saint Paul-based writer. He is the author of numerous children's books, including picture books, chapter books, and graphic novels. When not hunched over his laptop, Brandon enjoys watching movies and television, reading, baseball, and spending every spare moment with his wife and their two children.

ABOUT THE BASKETBALL STARS

LeBron James has been a dominating force on the court since the Cleveland Cavaliers drafted him first overall straight out of high school. He averages more than 25 points per game, along with 7 rebounds and 7 assists.

Nickname: King James, LBJ, Chosen One (to name a few)

Years in the NBA: 12 (2003–present)

Teams: Cavaliers and Heat

Position: Small Forward/Shooting Guard

Chris Paul is the model of what a point guard should be. While he can score with ease, averaging almost 20 points per game, it's his league-leading assist total that makes him an integral part of his team. He is also one of the NBA's leaders in steals.

Nickname: CP3

Years in the NBA: 10

Teams: Hornets and Clippers

Position: Point Guard

John Stockton averaged double-digit points and assists throughout his career, which earned him 10 trips to the NBA All-Star Game. He is the all-time NBA leader in both assists (15,806) and steals (3,265).

Nickname: Stock

Years in the NBA: 19

Team: Jazz

Position: Point Guard

THINK ABOUT IT

1. When Carter says he is having a difficult time making friends at his new school, were you surprised or not? Why or why not? Use examples in the story to explain your answer.

2. Carter is a great basketball player, but he is new to the team. Do you feel it is fair that Coach Horton puts him in a starting role and creates plays for him right away? Be sure to explain your answer.

3. Read another Game On! story. In *Pass for the Basket*, Ben plays basketball and helps his team to victory against the Eagle Valley Cougars. What role does Ben play in the other story? Is he the main character, or is the story about someone else? Compare the way Ben helps his team in each of the stories.

WRITE ABOUT IT

1. At first, Ben is jealous of Carter's role on the basketball team. Have you ever been jealous of anyone? Write a story about it. Describe what caused you to be jealous, and how you reacted to it.

2. Sal gives Ben a jersey to help inspire him after a difficult loss. Is there something, like a lucky charm or a favorite song, or someone, like a grandparent or hero, that inspires you? Describe this thing or person. What do you find inspiring about it or them?

3. Imagine that you play on the Grizzlies' basketball team. What's your position? Are you a starter? Write a story about a game where you help your team win. Do you score the last basket or block a shot? Remember, there are many ways to help your team win a game.

GET YOUR GAME ON!

Read more about Ben and his friends as they get their game on.

Eyes on the Puck
Goalie Annie Roger learns she needs prescription glasses, and her confidence is shattered. Will a visit to Sal's Used Sporting Goods be enough to help Annie see things differently?

Race Down the Slopes
Blinded by a crush, Gabe Santiago accepts an invitation to join the ski team even though he has never skied slalom before. Will a pair of goggles from Sal's Used Sporting Goods prove to be Gabe's lucky charm?

Strike Out the Side
Logan Parrish has a great fastball, but hitters are starting to figure him out. After a devastating loss, Logan goes searching for a new pitch. Will it be enough to help Logan in the big game?